## CONTRASTS IN METHODIST ARCHITECTURE

*Interior of the new Methodist Church at Banstead, Surrey (above) and one of the early Methodist places of worship - Denham Methodist Church (left)*

*Although the progress of Christianity through the ages has been marked by many men who were willing to die for their faith, John Wesley was a man who lived for his faith, professing it with such vigour that he became a legend in his own lifetime. His story is also that of the world-wide Methodist Church, for it is founded on his work and ideas.*

Acknowledgment

*Photographs on the front endpapers are from the Keith Ellis Collection (Denham Methodist Church) and from Photo Reportage Ltd (Banstead Methodist Church).*

*The publishers also wish to acknowledge the help of the* Methodist Recorder.

# John Wesley
*Founder of Methodism*

by JOHN A VICKERS BA BD
with illustrations by RONALD JACKSON MSIA

Ladybird Books Ltd  Loughborough  1977

'Fire!' A cry of alarm rang through the Epworth Rectory one night in the winter of 1709. The family woke to find the thatched roof alight and the house filled with smoke. Between them, the rector and his wife and servants hurried the children downstairs and out into the garden, only to find that one of them, little Jacky, was missing.

The rector tried to fight his way back into the blazing house, but in vain. Again and again he was driven back. Then a small figure appeared against the glow of the flames at an upstairs window. Jacky Wesley had awakened to find himself alone in the house with the rafters above his head ablaze. He groped his way to the head of the stairs, only to find them in flames. He was trapped. But even at five and a half John Wesley knew

how to keep his head in a crisis. Dragging a chest to the bedroom window, he clambered on it and was spotted by someone in the yard below.

There was no time to fetch a ladder and his plight seemed desperate. Then someone had an idea and ran forward, calling on one of his companions to follow him. One of them climbed on the shoulders of the other and in this way could just reach the window sill. Jacky was rescued, but only just in time, for a few moments later the blazing roof crashed in.

The Wesley family had lost everything and were homeless until the rectory was rebuilt. But what did it matter, so long as everyone was safe?

5

*Susanna Wesley and her family*

Jacky Wesley was the second of Samuel Wesley's three sons at the time of this dramatic rescue. His mother was convinced that it was God's doing. She called him, in the words of the Bible, 'a brand plucked from the burning' and felt that God must have some special work for him to do. So she resolved that she would take even more care of Jacky than of her other children.

Susanna Wesley was a firm but devoted mother. She undertook the education of her ten children and arranged for each of them to have six hours of lessons a day from the time they were five. Even the girls were included, at a time when the education of girls was almost unheard of. Susanna set aside a time every week when she could talk with each of them in turn. She insisted on obedience and good manners, especially to the

servants. She did not believe it was kind to spoil a child and one of the first things Jacky Wesley was taught was to cry quietly. (No one has ever discovered how she managed to do this!) But she knew that encouragement is worth far more than penalties and if any of them had done wrong they were never punished provided they owned up and showed that they were really sorry.

Epworth was a remote and inaccessible parish among the Lincolnshire fens. The village folk did not take kindly to outsiders and were hostile to their scholarly rector with his high principles and determined manner. They burned his crops and maimed his cattle and even got him gaoled in Lincoln Castle for a small debt. So life was difficult for the Wesleys, but they were a happy and united family.

When he was ten, John Wesley left the Lincolnshire fens and travelled all the way to London to become a boarder at Charterhouse School. He had been nominated by the Duke of Buckingham as a *Gownboy* (a boy who received his education free upon being nominated by one of the Governors of Charterhouse). His older brother Samuel was a master at Westminster School and two years later the baby of the family, Charles, went to Westminster also, as a scholar. So for four years all three Wesley brothers were in London together.

Life at Charterhouse was tough, especially for the younger boys. The seniors stole their food and John Wesley remembered his schooldays as a time when he often had very little to eat except bread. His lessons included Latin, Greek and Hebrew – but not modern languages, which he taught himself later in life. As a Gownboy he had to get up at 5 o'clock every morning and he started each day by dutifully running three times round the school garden before breakfast, as his father had advised him.

Looking back on his schooldays, he was sure that they helped to make him so healthy and able to endure hardship later on.

Epworth was much too far away for him to visit, even in the holidays, but letters went to and fro, and he heard all the family news – including the 'ghost' which his sisters nicknamed 'Old Jeffrey'. Nowadays visitors to the Old Rectory may sleep in the long attic room at the top of the house without hearing anything unusual, but for two months from the beginning of December 1716, the Wesley family were disturbed by many strange noises – groans, knockings, the smashing of glass or the crash of pewter pots – and, less often, by strange sights too. John Wesley checked their reports with great care and was convinced that here was proof of the supernatural.

*Gownboys' room, Charterhouse*

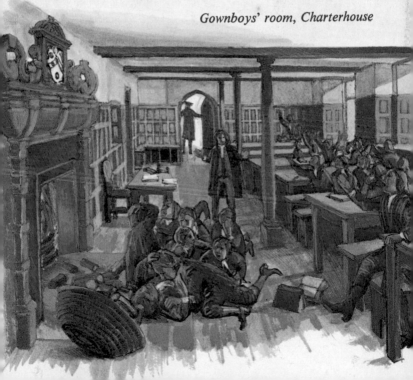

At the age of 17 John left school for Oxford with a scholarship of £40 a year. The next six years, while he was a student at Christ Church under the shadow of the Cathedral Church and 'Tom Tower', were full of both work and enjoyment. There was always good company and conversation in the coffee houses and taverns of the town. When he was not either reading or talking, Wesley spent much of his spare time playing chess, backgammon, billiards, tennis and other games. He was too poor to own or hire a horse, but sometimes he would set out to walk over the Cotswold hills to visit his friends the Kirkhams at Stanton Rectory near Evesham. There too he fell in love for the first time.

At the same time he was beginning to take life more seriously. He decided to become an Anglican priest like his father, and was ordained deacon in 1725 and priest in 1728. He also began

*John Wesley relaxes at an Oxford coffee house*

to keep a diary, noting down carefully how he spent both his time and his money each day. He used a complicated mixture of shorthand and code which has only recently been deciphered. He kept up this practice for the rest of his life.

These years at Oxford left their mark on Wesley in other ways. Even at the height of his career as a popular evangelist, he was still an Oxford don, logical in thought, clear in argument and able to quote from authors he had read as a student many years before. In 1726 the news reached his family at Epworth that he had been made a Fellow of Lincoln College, which meant that from now on he would have an assured income as a tutor. His academic career seemed well launched and his father, still struggling to make ends meet, wrote proudly: 'Wherever I am, my Jack is Fellow of Lincoln.'

Charles Wesley was a lively and sociable young man when he joined his brother in Oxford in 1726. He was determined to enjoy his student days to the full and declared that he was in no hurry to be 'made a saint'. Soon afterwards, John left the university and went back to Lincolnshire for two years to help his father in his parish work. When he returned in 1729, he found that his debonair young brother had sobered down and was one of a small group of students who had begun to meet regularly in one another's rooms to study the Bible and pray. Such behaviour seemed very strange to their fellow students, who gave them various nicknames such as 'Bible moths', 'the Holy Club' and 'Methodists'. It was this last label which stuck and was transferred in due course to John Wesley's later followers.

John Wesley soon became recognised as a leader among these serious-minded young men. Besides meeting together and attending the sacrament of Holy Communion much more regularly than was then the custom, they began to show a practical concern for the poor. At a time when there were no social services or welfare state, they found time to visit the prisons and the poorer parts of the town. They put aside some of their money to buy food, clothing and medicines to distribute among the destitute and started a school for the children of poor families. All this was an attempt to obey what Jesus called the second commandment, 'Thou shalt love thy neighbour as thyself.' John Wesley himself found that he could live on £28 a year, so he began to give away the rest of his income.

*John Wesley preaching to prisoners at Bocardo Prison, Oxford*

Georgia was a new colony on the Atlantic coast of North America. Its founder, General James Oglethorpe, was devoted to a variety of philanthropic causes, including prison reform. He intended the colony to be a refuge for discharged debtors and other 'rough diamonds' from English prisons, and also for the victims of religious persecution in Europe. So its first settlers were a strange assortment of saints and gaol-birds.

The two Wesley brothers met General Oglethorpe in the summer of 1735 and by the end of the year they were already on board the *Simmonds* and on their way to Georgia. John was to serve as parish priest at Savannah, the main settlement, and Charles as Oglethorpe's secretary. John had a romantic idea of life in the New World and imagined himself as a missionary to the Indians. But life in the raw new settlement of Savannah was hard and Wesley soon found himself caught up in the petty squabbles and rivalries of the colony.

Most of the settlers had no time for the strict rules and piety of this prim little Oxford don. Worse still, he got involved in a love affair with the niece of the storekeeper at Savannah, one of the most influential men in the settlement. Sophy Hopkey showed herself a willing disciple and obviously found him an acceptable suitor. But John could not make up his mind about marrying her and in the end she got tired of waiting and married someone else.

The tensions between Wesley and the other settlers were brought to a head by this affair and his clumsy handling of the situation. One day, because he was unsure about her sincerity, he unwisely refused to admit her to the Sacrament. This brought a storm of protest about his ears. A series of charges were brought against him and he had to escape from the colony. Soon he was following his brother back to England, only two years after they had set out with such high hopes.

*Refusing the Sacrament to Sophy Hopkey
in Savannah, Georgia*

15

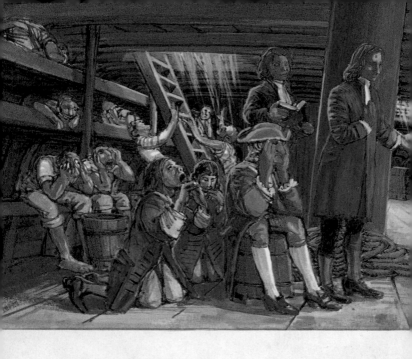

The Georgia venture had been a dismal failure, but the Wesley brothers did learn some important things from it. In the life of a sheltered community like Oxford they were accepted and had a place. But in the wider world were problems and situations with which they did not know how to deal. So they arrived back in England in humbler mood.

In particular, one incident from their voyage out to Georgia two years before stuck in their minds. Among the passengers aboard the *Simmonds* were a number of German families. They were members of a pious and industrious group known as the Moravians who were seeking to start a new life in America. In mid-Atlantic the little sailing ship was lashed by fierce winter gales for days on end. Enormous seas pounded its timbers

*The courageous Moravians singing psalms*

and poured below decks. The mainsail was torn to ribbons. At the height of the storm, even the hardiest of the sailors were in terror of their lives and the Wesley brothers discovered that, face to face with death, they themselves were as cowardly as anyone. So much for their faith in God and his providence!

But in the midst of the general panic and the uproar of the wind and waves the Moravians calmly went on singing their psalms. Even their women and children seemed unafraid of death. John Wesley marvelled at their courage and realised that these German peasants with their simple faith in God had a secret for which he was still seeking when he arrived back in London two years later. There, at last, the moment of discovery arrived for both brothers.

On Whit Sunday 1738, Charles Wesley lay in bed in the home of a friend, recovering from an illness. Suddenly he was filled with an overwhelming sense of God's love. Three days later and very near the same spot John too found what he had been looking for. It was his 'spiritual birthday' and he never forgot the events of that day. His account of it is the best known of all the passages in his famous *Journal*.

When he awoke that morning, May 24th 1738, he opened his Bible and his eye fell on words which seemed full of meaning for him: 'Thou are not far from the kingdom of God.' Later on he went to St Paul's Cathedral to hear evensong and remembered that the words of the anthem which the choir sang were: 'Out of the deep have I called unto Thee, O Lord.'

This seemed to be just what he himself was doing. Then in the evening he went – 'very unwillingly,' he says – to a meeting of a little group of Christians in a house in Aldersgate Street. Here, while someone was reading aloud from the writings of Martin Luther, the great German reformer, John Wesley felt his heart 'strangely warmed' by the love of God. 'I felt I did trust in Christ, Christ alone, for salvation; and an assurance was given me that He had taken away *my* sins, even mine, and saved me from the law of sin and death.'

George Whitefield, the son of a Gloucester innkeeper, had been one of the younger members of the Holy Club at Oxford. He was a preacher of fiery eloquence and by the time the Wesleys returned from Georgia he was already well known as an evangelist on both sides of the Atlantic. Early in 1739 he was in Bristol where, like Wesley, he found many of the churches shut against him. So he began to preach in the open air.

In the eighteenth century this was a very great novelty. Some people were shocked and thought it vulgar and dangerous. But many, especially among the poorer classes, who never went inside a church, flocked to hear Whitefield preach. The miners of Kingswood, just outside Bristol, were rough, uneducated men, but they listened eagerly to his passionate words. The idea that God loved them as much as the wealthy and the respectable made the tears run down their blackened cheeks. Whitefield had promised to return shortly to America, but he could not abandon such people as these. He wrote to Wesley begging him to come from London and help him.

Wesley went, but full of misgivings. For a clergyman to preach anywhere except in church seemed to him almost unthinkable. But he stood and listened as Whitefield preached in the open air. He saw the effects of Whitefield's work and was reminded that Jesus himself had once preached his 'Sermon on the Mount'.

*George Whitefield preaching to the miners of Kingswood, Bristol*

Soon his hesitation was ended and he was taking up his new career as a 'field-preacher'. The decision shaped the course of the rest of his life and for the next fifty years he was to travel endlessly through every part of the British Isles.

All over England there are places which are still pointed out as one of the spots on which John Wesley once preached. Often he chose the market place or village green, where there was room for people to gather. Many are marked today by a plaque. He would stand on the steps of the village cross, or on a wall or a cart, so that people could both see and hear him better. At Gwennap, near Redruth in Cornwall, he found a great hollow in the ground which served as a natural amphitheatre in which hundreds could hear him. In the Staffordshire town of Wednesbury he stood on the steps of a malt-house; the building has long since been pulled down, but the steps, known as Wesley's 'horseblock', have been lovingly preserved.

In 1742, seven years after his father's death, he revisited Epworth. He offered to preach in the parish church, but was rebuffed. So he waited till the church service had ended and then preached from his father's tombstone in the churchyard. As a preacher, he was much less emotional and dramatic than Whitefield, but many in his audience felt as though he had singled them out from the rest and spoke to them alone, knowing their thoughts and needs.

Although his principle was 'to go to those who needed him most', Wesley did not only preach to the poor. The wealthy and fashionable were also 'children of God' and needed the gospel just as much.

*Wesley preaching from his father's tombstone*

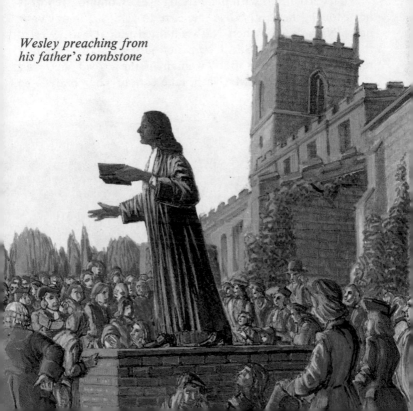

Eighteenth-century Bath was a centre of fashion and high life; and the so-called 'King of Bath' was Beau Nash, a notoriously foppish figure. One day, while Wesley was preaching in the town, Nash threw down a challenge. 'By what authority do you do these things?' he asked.

'By the authority of Jesus Christ,' answered Wesley. Nash replied that Wesley was breaking the law by holding his open-air meetings, and also that he was frightening people out of their wits. 'Sir,' said Wesley, 'did you ever hear me preach?' Nash admitted that he hadn't, but was judging 'by common report.'

Wesley fixed him with his piercing eyes. 'Common report is not enough,' he said. 'Give me leave to ask, Sir, is not your name Nash?' And when Nash admitted that it was, Wesley thrust home with: 'Sir, I *dare* not judge *you* by common report.' But it was a poor woman in the crowd who had the last word. 'You, Mr Nash, take care of your body,' she

said. 'We take care of our souls; and for the food of our souls we come here.'

Before he left Bristol in the spring of 1739, Wesley undertook the building of a school for the children of the Kingswood miners and also laid the foundations of a chapel in the Horse-fair, with accommodation for himself and his fellow-preachers and stabling for their horses. The 'New Room', as it is still called, was largely rebuilt a few years later, but still stands as the 'oldest Methodist church in the world'.

*Challenged by Beau Nash*

Bristol became Wesley's headquarters in the west of England and one of the three bases from which he set out on his many journeys. The others were Newcastle in the north and London. To the north of Moorfields just outside the City of London stood the shell of a building which had once been the royal cannon foundry. In 1716 it was shattered by an explosion. A new Royal Arsenal was established at Woolwich and the old foundry stood empty and roofless for over twenty years. Then in 1739 Wesley bought it for £115 and spent another £700 on repairs. The chapel held 1,500, with men and women seated separately. It became the nearest thing Wesley had to a 'home'. His mother spent her closing years there and was buried nearby in Bunhill Fields, the famous nonconformist burial ground, along with John Bunyan, Daniel Defoe and William Blake.

*Thomas Maxfield preaching at the Foundery*

In the spring of 1740 Wesley left a young man named Thomas Maxfield in charge at the 'Foundery' while he was busy in Bristol. Because there was no clergyman available, Maxfield took it upon himself to preach at the services although he was not ordained. Wesley was still a high-churchman who believed that there were some things which only a priest could do. So he was deeply shocked by the news and came riding back to the Foundery in great haste. But the first person he met there was his mother, who was ready for him with words of warning. 'My son,' she said, 'take care what you do. Thomas Maxfield is as much called to preach the gospel as ever you were!' She persuaded him to hear Maxfield preach before he took any further action. Wesley did so and had to admit that it was God's doing. 'Who am I that I should withstand God?' he asked. So Thomas Maxfield became the first Methodist lay preacher.

*A Methodist 'class' meeting is threatened*

By the end of the year there were twenty lay preachers helping Wesley. As the work grew, he employed more and more of them as his 'Assistants' and stationed them in different parts of the country. They came from many walks of life. John Nelson was a stone-mason from Yorkshire; Sampson Staniforth, a soldier who had served in Flanders and Germany; Silas Told, a sailor with gruesome memories of the slave trade; John Pawson, a farmer's son. Others had been schoolmasters. Although some were of quite humble origin, none of them were uneducated. Wesley set them high standards, encouraging them to learn Greek and Hebrew so that they could read the Bible in the original languages; and several of them became better scholars than most of the clergy. But he chose them chiefly for their experience of God and for their strength of character.

Although he remained an Anglican priest, Wesley never had a parish of his own. He said that he looked upon the whole world as his parish and claimed that, as a Fellow of an Oxford College, he was free to preach wherever he chose. Many of the clergy, however, naturally resented the way in which he 'trespassed' on their parishes and preached there without their permission. This was one cause of the hostility towards Wesley and his followers. Another was the suspicion aroused by the way in which the Methodists met privately in small groups called 'classes'. They did so to share their religious experience and to help each other to live better Christian lives. But some of their neighbours suspected them of plotting to overthrow the government; and in 1745, at the time of the Young Pretender's invasion of England, word went round that the Methodists were 'papists' and Jacobites in disguise.

29

Mobs were raised against them, often incited by local clergy and gentry. They were beaten up and dragged through the gutters, and their homes were ransacked and wrecked.

Wesley himself learned how to face a mob with calm bravery. His method was to go into the middle of the mob and confront the ring-leader. One day a drunken crowd burst into the house in which he was staying in Falmouth. His friends tried to persuade him to hide, but Wesley refused. Instead, he stepped forward resolutely into their midst, asking, 'Which of you has anything to say to me? To which of you have I done any wrong?' His enemies fell back, shamefaced.

One of the ugliest situations he ever faced was at Wednesbury on 20th October 1743. The local mob had been on the rampage for weeks and Wesley had come to support and encourage his suffering followers. That afternoon the mob twice surrounded the house where he was, demanding to have 'the minister'. Wesley sent for their leader and several others and talked with them until they changed their tune and swore that they would defend him with their own lives. He then agreed to go with them to the home of a neighbouring magistrate, Mr Lane, but he was in no hurry to get involved. They found that he had hastily retired to bed and would not see them.

Going on to the neighbouring town of Walsall, they met with the same response from the magistrate there. By now they were growing tired, but just as they were setting out for home a rival mob came pouring down upon them. This mob seized Wesley and carried him off as their prize. It was late in the evening before he got safely back to Wednesbury. He had been at the mercy of the mob for six hours or more, but escaped unharmed except for a torn waistcoat and some skin from one of his hands.

*At the mercy of the mob*

Even when it did not come to open violence, many different ways of silencing him were tried. Sometimes they rang the church bells to drown his voice. At Pensford in Somerset a maddened bull was driven into the crowd that stood listening to him on the village green, but again and again it swerved away from where he stood. Wesley recorded one amusing incident with relish. A heckler at Bedford had come with a pocketful of rotten eggs ready to throw at the preacher. But before he could do so, someone clapped his hands over the man's pockets, with disastrous results. 'In an instant,' wrote Wesley, 'he was perfumed all over, though it was not as sweet as balsam.'

For nearly fifty years Wesley rode up and down England, through wind, rain and snow. The pages of his *Journal* are as full of weather as they are of place-names. He was always impatient of delays, eager to reach his next congregation. Once, while held up at Holyhead by stormy weather, his impatience with the captain and crew of the boat that should have been taking him across to Ireland made him rewrite an old rhyme:

There are, unless my memory fail,
Five causes why we should not sail:
The fog is thick, the wind is high;
It rains, or may do by and by;
Or – any other reason why!

The England through which he rode was one of small country towns and villages still largely isolated from one another. Much of the common land was still unenclosed. The unsurfaced roads were often almost impassable. Carriages easily overturned or stuck fast, and Wesley found horseback much faster and safer. He often rode with the reins lying loose on his horse's neck, believing that left to itself the horse would not stumble. And to use his time to the full, he read as he went along. In his closing years, when he could no longer ride, he fitted out his carriage with bookshelves and a portable desk, so that he could continue to write letters and edit his books as he journeyed.

London, with a population of three-quarters of a million, was the only city of any size at that time, followed a long way behind by Bristol and Norwich. The effects of the Industrial Revolution were only just beginning to be felt in the Midlands and North. But Wesley spent much of his time in the new industrial areas with their growing population of workers. He watched Birmingham grow from a village into a thriving manufacturing town of 60,000. And on the banks of the Severn in 1779 he saw the first cast-iron bridge in the world being erected where it now gives its name to the village of Ironbridge. He compared it with the Colossus of Rhodes, one of the wonders of the ancient world; but in fact, though he

only half realised it, he was witnessing the birth of the modern technological age.

Wesley must have ridden more miles and paid more tolls than any other man of his century. Yet, so far as we know, he was never held up by a highwayman. Perhaps the word got round that his saddlebags contained nothing more valuable than a change of clothing and a supply of his religious tracts.

*Wesley and John Fletcher, the parish priest at Madeley, admire the new iron bridge*

It is hardly surprising that when John Wesley eventually married, it was not a success. He declared that he would not let his marriage cause him to travel one mile less or preach one fewer sermon.

*John Wesley's brother Charles is shown here composing one of his many hymns which are now famous throughout the world*

His wife, a well-to-do London widow, nursed him back to health after an accident and they were married very soon afterwards. At first Mrs Wesley accompanied her husband on his travels, but she soon grew tired of sharing the hardships of the road. She was jealous by nature and resented having to take second place to his work.

His brother Charles, on the other hand, was very happily married. He did not travel as widely as John, but settled first in Bristol and later in London and gave his support to the work there. When he died in 1788, he was buried at Marylebone Old Church, where a memorial to him can still be seen. But his real memorial is in the many hymns he wrote.

He has been called 'the sweet singer of Methodism' and he put into verse the radiant experience of the early Methodists. Many of his hymns, such as 'Love divine, all loves excelling', 'Hark, the herald angels sing' and 'Christ the Lord is risen today', are now familiar throughout the Christian world and are found in almost every hymn book.

His two sons proved to be musical prodigies, whose recitals were much talked of in London society; and his grandson was the great organist and composer Samuel Sebastian Wesley.

Although John Wesley was at ease among men of most levels of society, he was often scathing in his comments on the behaviour of the wealthy upper classes. One thing he could not tolerate, in others any more than in himself, was idleness. Among his friends was the great writer Dr Samuel Johnson, who said that Wesley could talk well on any subject – a high compliment, coming from such an outstanding conversationalist. But in one respect at least the two men were very different. Wesley filled every hour of his day with useful activity and was punctual to the minute. 'John Wesley's conversation is good,' Johnson complained, 'but he is never at leisure. He is always obliged to go at a certain hour. This is very disagreeable to a man who loves to fold his legs and have out his talk, as I do.'

Wesley too was a man of letters. He wrote many books and pamphlets, edited many more and was his own publisher, with his preachers as the booksellers. Besides many sermons, hymn books and other religious works, he wrote a history of England, textbooks for his schools and pamphlets giving his views on everything from tea-drinking to 'the cause and cure of earthquakes'. One of Johnson's most famous works was a great English Dictionary. Wesley also compiled a dictionary. With his tongue 'in his cheek' he claimed it was not only 'the best English Dictionary in the World' but also the shortest and cheapest. It was intended not for the educated classes, but for the many ordinary folk who never went to school – 'persons of common sense and no learning', as he called them.

The old 'Foundery' was Wesley's London headquarters for forty years. It was a centre for many different activities besides preaching. Wesley started a school for the children of the poor, with two teachers and sixty scholars. He built an almshouse for homeless paupers. He and his preachers made their home there whenever they were in London. All the residents at the Foundery ate their meals together as one family.

*Dr Johnson enjoyed John Wesley's company*

In 1745 Wesley opened London's first free clinic and dispensary there. Medical science was then in the hands of quacks and amateurs. There were very few skilled doctors and the poor could not afford to go to them. Wesley employed an apothecary and a surgeon, so that the poor could come to the Foundery and obtain treatment and medicines. In 1747 he published a little book which proved more popular than anything else he wrote. It was called *Primitive Physick or an Easy and Natural Method of curing Most Diseases*. This was a collection of popular remedies for all kinds of illness. Wesley's method was a simple one. He included remedies which he or other people he knew had tried and which seemed to work.

*Experimenting with electric shocks*

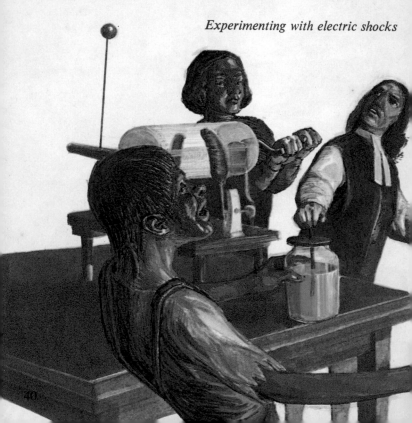

Many of his 'cures' seem very strange to us. Bruises were to be treated with treacle spread on brown paper, and baldness could be cured by rubbing the scalp with a mixture of honey and onions! But he also recommended fresh air, exercise and good simple food.

Several people, including Benjamin Franklin in America, were experimenting with a mysterious force called 'electricity' as a cure for all sorts of illness. Wesley published a simplified version of Franklin's book about electricity, and he bought a machine with which he was able to give electric shocks to his patients. He tried it out – on himself as well as on others – with considerable success. You can still see his machine in his house in London.

*John Wesley with Mr Samuel Tooth,
local preacher and builder of the new chapel*

By 1777 the time had come for the Foundery to be replaced. John Wesley was growing old, though he still travelled around the country and got up regularly at 4 o'clock in the morning. He still had enemies, but more and more was looked upon as a veteran evangelist. More and more people joined the Methodist society in London and many of them were well-to-do and respectable folk.

So in April 1777, Wesley laid the foundation stone of a new chapel 'in the City Road' opposite Bunhill Fields and just beyond the open space called Moorfields. The chapel was opened in November 1778. It was an elegant and well-proportioned building which showed that Methodism was becoming accepted in the upper levels of society. The pillars supporting the gallery were made from masts given to him by King George III from the naval dockyard at Deptford.

Wesley also built himself a house at one side of the chapel. It still stands there and contains many of his belongings. Here is the portable writing desk that accompanied him on his

journeys, with the sand-sprinkler which he used in the days before blotting paper; the walnut bureau with its secret compartments in which he used to hide his confidential letters; the gallon teapot designed and made for him by an admirer, the great master potter Josiah Wedgwood; his preaching gown and bands, reminding us how short he was; his electrical machine, and some of the many books he wrote and edited.

This was Wesley's home for the last twelve years of his life, though he was often away from it for months at a time. He came back to it for the last time early in 1791, to die in his four-poster bed, like the one that still stands in a back room there.

John Wesley was so busy preaching to the people of England and organising his societies that for over forty years he never went outside the British Isles. Then he took a holiday in Holland. But in the meantime his movement had begun to spread to other parts of the world.

In 1757 a well-to-do planter from the island of Antigua in the West Indies read one of Wesley's books and was so impressed by it that he set out for England in order to meet its author. His name was Nathaniel Gilbert. Wesley preached in his London home to the Gilbert family, their servants and slaves, and sowed seeds of faith that soon began to grow.

As soon as he returned to Antigua, Gilbert himself began to preach. He would gather together the slaves from his plantation and talk to them about the love of God and the joy and peace it had brought into his life. He did not set them free, partly because the island's laws were very harsh towards freed slaves; but he began to care for them and seek their welfare. From this small seed grew Methodism's work overseas.

Wesley had no intention of starting a new Church. He wanted to bring new life to the Church of England and encouraged his followers to worship at their parish churches. But some of the steps he took were contrary to the practices of the Church of England. We have seen how he employed laymen as preachers, organised his followers into 'societies' with strict rules of membership, and built his own 'preaching-houses'. In 1784 he took a more serious step, when he ordained some of his preachers to go out to America.

Methodism first came to America about 1776, nearly ten years after Nathaniel Gilbert had returned home to Antigua. It started among Irish immigrants in New York and, about the same time, among the farmers of Maryland. Wesley sent some of his preachers out to help them. But by the early 1770s trouble was brewing between Britain and her American colonies and in 1775 open war broke out. As a result, the thirteen colonies became independent and the United States of America was born.

*Wesley preaching to Nathaniel Gilbert*
*and his family, servants and slaves*

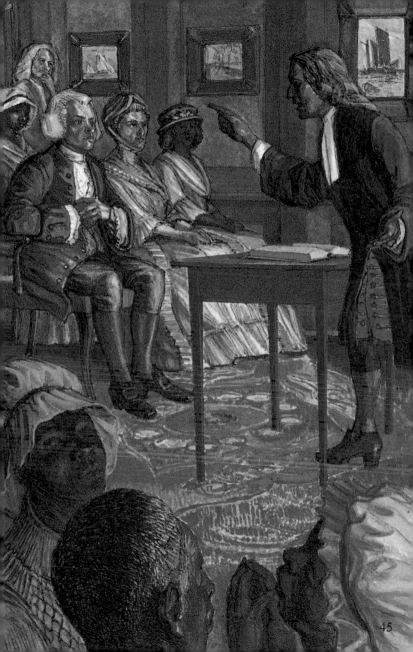

The war affected the Methodists considerably. By the end of it all the preachers who had come out from England had returned home, except for one, Francis Asbury, who became the leader of the American Methodists. Most of the Anglican clergy had also returned home, leaving the American settlers without spiritual leadership. John Wesley tried to persuade the Bishop of London to ordain preachers for America, but there were political and legal difficulties, because the colonists had rebelled against British rule.

*Thomas Coke ordains Francis Asbury at the Lovely Lane Chapel, Baltimore, 1784*

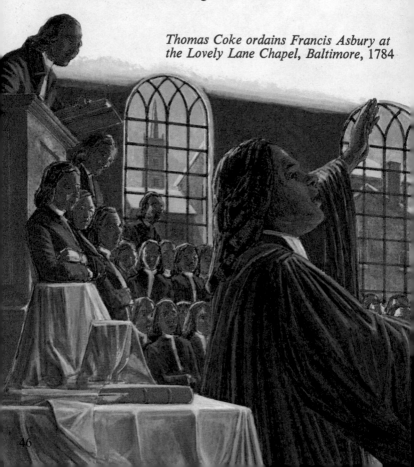

In the end, Wesley took matters into his own hands. In the Church of England, only a bishop can make men into priests by ordaining them. Wesley, from his study of the history of the Church, believed that in the early days of Christianity priests and bishops had been the same; so, as a priest in the Church of England, he had the power to ordain others.

So in 1784, after the war, he ordained three of his preachers to provide ministers for the American Methodists. One, a young Welshman named Thomas Coke, was already a clergyman. Wesley ordained him as 'superintendent' of the new Church and he in turn ordained Francis Asbury. In this way Wesley tried to provide for the spiritual needs of the American people at an important time in their history. The separate American Methodist Church then formed has grown into one of the largest Protestant Churches in the United States.

*Wesley at Winchelsea, aged 87*

Although he believed that his actions were justified by circumstances and the needs of the American people, Wesley was widely criticised for abandoning the Church of England and its rules. He always protested his loyalty to the Church in which he had been brought up, but he has sometimes been described as like a rower, looking in one direction but travelling in the other. After his death, his followers in England found it difficult to decide whether they still belonged to the Church of England or not. The Anglican leaders, too, were not at all sure that they wanted to have anything to do with these enthusiastic Methodists. So before long the two drifted apart and Methodism became a separate Church, as in America. By the 1830s, when the Oxford Movement began to bring new life into the Church of England, the gap had already grown too wide for the Methodists to bridge.

On his 80th birthday John Wesley was in Holland and wrote: 'I have this day lived fourscore years; and by the mercy of God, my eyes are not waxed dim. And what little strength of body or mind I had thirty years since, just the same I have now. God grant I may never live to be useless!'

That prayer was granted. He lived to be almost 88, but he continued to rise at 4 a m and kept up his travelling and his preaching almost to the end. At one side of the churchyard at Winchelsea in Sussex stands an ash tree which marks the spot where he preached for the last time in the open air. So many events and sermons had been crowded into the fifty years since he first stood up to speak out of doors to the people of Bristol. He was now within five months of his death, but even so he had not yet done. His very last sermon was not preached until February 23rd 1791, in a house in Leatherhead.

The next day he sat down to write a letter to a young Member of Parliament called William Wilberforce, who had recently begun his long campaign to abolish the slave trade. Wesley had been an opponent of slavery for many years. He called it 'that execrable villainy which is the scandal of religion, of England, and of human nature.' As long ago as 1774 he had written a strong attack on it called *Thoughts upon Slavery*. Now Wesley wrote to encourage the younger man. He knew it would not be an easy victory. ' . . . Unless God has raised you up for this very thing,' he wrote, 'you will be worn out by the opposition of men and devils. But if God be for you, who can be against you? Are all of them together stronger than God? O be not weary of well doing! Go on, in the name of God and in the power of His might, till even American slavery (the vilest that ever saw the sun) shall vanish away before it . . . That He who has guided you from youth up may continue to strengthen you in this and all things is the prayer of,

> dear Sir,
> Your affectionate servant,
> John Wesley.'

These may well have been the very last words John Wesley wrote. How they must have been cherished by Wilberforce as a source of encouragement until the slave trade was eventually abolished in 1807. Meanwhile, back in his home in the City Road John Wesley lay dying, with some of his closest friends gathered around him. Not long before the end, on March 2nd 1791, he rallied the little strength he had left to repeat several times, 'The best of all is – God is with us!'

No one in 18th century England was so well known among people of every class of society. Ten thousand people filed past his coffin and his funeral had to be held before dawn for fear of unmanageable crowds. The tireless traveller had come to the end of his long road at last.

# INDEX

*Page*

America    14, 16, 21, 41, 44, 46, 47, 48
Antigua    44
Architecture, Methodist
    *front endpapers*
Asbury, Francis    46, 47

Baltimore    46
Bath    24
Bedford    32
Birmingham    34
Blake, William    26
Bocardo Prison, Oxford    12-13
Bristol    21, 25, 26, 27, 34, 37, 49
Bunyan, John    26

Charterhouse School    8, 9
Christ Church, Oxford    10
City Road Chapel    42, 43, 50
Coffee house, Oxford    10-11
Coke, Thomas    46, 47
Cornwall    22
Cotswold Hills    10

Defoe, Daniel    26
Deptford    42

Electricity    41
Epworth    7, 9, 11, 23
Epworth Rectory    4, 9
Evesham    10

Falmouth    30
Flanders    28
Fletcher, John    35
Foundery (chapel)    26, 27, 38, 40, 42
Franklin, Benjamin    41

George III, King    42
Georgia    14, 16, 21

*Page*

Germany    16, 17, 19, 28
Gilbert, Nathaniel    44, 45
Gloucester    21
Gwennap    22

Holland    43, 49
'Holy Club' (Oxford)    12, 21
Holyhead    32
Hopkey, Sophy    14, 15
Horsefair (Bristol)    25
Hymns    36, 37

Ireland    32
Ironbridge    34
Iron bridge, first    34-35

Johnson, Dr Samuel    38, 39
*Journal*    18, 32

Kingswood (Bristol)    21, 25

Lay preachers    27-29
Leatherhead    49
Lincoln Castle    7
Lincolnshire    7, 8, 12
London    8, 17, 20, 21, 26, 34, 37, 38, 40, 41, 44
London, Bishop of    46
Lovely Lane Chapel
    (Baltimore)    46-47
Luther, Martin    19

Magistrates    30
Maryland    44
Marylebone Old Church    37
Maxfield, Thomas    26, 27
Medical treatment    40-41
Methodists    12, 28, 29, 30, 37, 42, 44, 46, 47, 48
Mob violence    30, 31, 32